W9-BQI-163

Ndito Runs

Laurie Halse Anderson

Illustrations by Anita van der Merwe

Henry Holt and Company • New York

Acknowledgments

The following people kindly worked with the author to ensure that Ndito's story was told accurately and with respect:

The support staff of Ambassador of the Republic of Kenya Benjamin Kipkorir, especially Secretary of Information William Meda and Beatrice Ngoe, assistant in the Information Department. Beatrice generously read and reread the manuscript and made valuable suggestions.

Brother Colm O'Connell, who teaches and coaches students at St. Patrick's High School in Iten, Kenya. Most children in the Kenyan highlands grow up running miles each day to get to school, and several have gone on to join the ranks of the fastest runners in the world. Brother O'Connell works to provide girls as well as boys the opportunity to become competitive athletes. He patiently answered countless questions with good humor.

Simone Kaplan of Henry Holt, who has a hard eye and a gentle manner. Thank you all very much.

Henry Holt and Company, Inc., *Publishers since 1866*
115 West 18th Street, New York, New York 10011
Henry Holt is a registered trademark of Henry Holt and Company, Inc.

Library of Congress Cataloging-in-Publication Data
Anderson, Laurie Halse.
Ndito runs / Laurie Halse Anderson;
illustrations by Anita van der Merwe.
Summary: A Kenyan girl runs past the thatch-covered homes
in her village, up the hillside, through the grassland, by the
water hole, on her way to school.
{1. Kenya—Fiction.   2. Blacks—Kenya—Fiction.   3. Running—Fiction.]
   I. Van der Merwe, Anita, ill.   II. Title.
PZ7.A54385Nd   1996   [E]—dc20   94-44649

ISBN 0-8050-3265-7
First Edition—1996
Printed in the United States of America on acid-free paper.∞
10 9 8 7 6 5 4 3 2 1

The artist used acrylic paint on canvas
to create the illustrations for this book.

To my parents, for letting me read instead of doing my chores; Greg, my husband and best friend, for his love and understanding; and my daughters, for raising the sun with laughter each morning

—L. H. A.

To Johan and Ancy

—A. V. D. M.

The morning sun warms the village. It is alive with people and animals. Ndito is going to school.

She greets the women carrying water pots.

She smiles at the children
playing in the shade.

She waves to Mama at the grinding stone.

She runs past Papa digging yams.

Ndito hurries away from the thatch-roofed, belly-shaped homes of her people. Her brothers thunder behind her. They call in loud voices and tease. The brother-boys laugh as they pass Ndito. They speed into the rising sun.

Ndito pays them no mind. Her strong feet sing fast in the dust as she races through the morning to school.

Ndito calls up animal dreams to keep
her company. She floats by the tall grass
like a gazelle.

She scampers over the savanna like a goat.

She hops under a baobab like a dik-dik.

She gallops up the hillside like a
wildebeest, her legs burning with speed.

Crowned cranes sweep across the sky.
Ndito shakes her crown of cocoa-colored
hair.

A young ostrich flutters her tail feathers. Ndito rustles her skirt.

Thousands of flamingos take to the air at the water hole. Ndito waves her arms in the pink breeze. She flies to school.

The smell of cattle rushes along the ridge. Ndito springs straight up like a warrior watching cattle.

The perfume of coffee beans trickles from a drying shed. Ndito twirls like a plump coffee bean.

The sun climbs high as Ndito
runs down the easy side of the hill.

A slow clump of brother-boys drag their tired feet. Ndito runs past them like an arrow. She smiles and tosses her head.

The schoolhouse roof shimmers in the heat. Ndito is almost there.

From the village she races, like a bird
she flies, on the wind she rises.

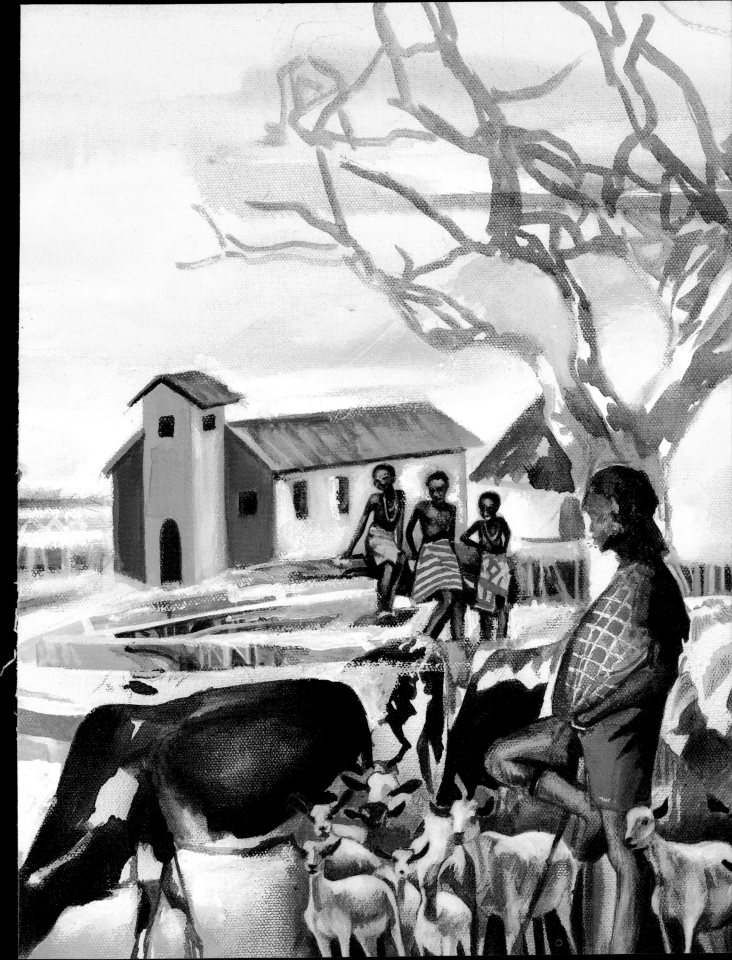

Through her Africa, across her Kenya,
over her highlands to school.